A Pony to Remember

CHARMING PONIES

A Pony
to
Remember

LOIS SZYMANSKI

HarperFestival®
A Division of HarperCollins Publishers

HarperCollins®, ▰®, and HarperFestival®
are trademarks of HarperCollins Publishers.

Charming Ponies: A Pony to Remember
Copyright © 1994 by Lois Knight Szymanski
Printed in the United States of America. All rights reserved.
No part of this book may be used or reproduced in any manner
whatsoever without written permission except in the case of
brief quotations embodied in critical articles and reviews. For
information address HarperCollins Children's Books, a division of
HarperCollins Publishers, 1350 Avenue of the Americas, New
York, NY 10019.
· www.harpercollinschildrens.com
Library of Congress catalog card number: 93-91020
ISBN 978-0-06-128870-8
Typography by Sasha Illingworth
❖
First HarperFestival edition, 2007
Originally published in 1994 as *New Kind of Magic*

This book is dedicated to the memory of
Rockerfritz, a tiny pony with a big heart, and to
Sam Kern for giving him to my children
when Rocky was just a tiny foal.

Acknowledgments

During the course of researching the legend of the lost Silver Mine of Silver Run, Maryland, I was privileged to find several resources that aided me. One was a column written by Ruth Seitler for *The Carroll County Times*. The other, a remarkable book entitled *Ghosts and Legends of Carroll County*, written by Jesse Glass and published by the Carroll County Public Library, offered immeasurable assistance. Parts of this book are quoted within the pages of *A Pony to Remember*. To both sources I wish to offer a special thank you.

A Pony to Remember

one

Jenny rubbed Magic's neck, and the black and white spotted pony moved closer, his head dropping as she scratched, until his nose was almost touching the ground.

"Feels good, doesn't it?" she asked him. "Come on, boy. I can't scratch you all night. Mom's probably already wondering what's taking me so long."

She rattled the can of oats, and Magic picked up

his step and followed her into the barn. She dumped the grain into his feed box and stood back as his nose made a dive. Magic would do anything for food. Jenny should know. She'd trained him to stand on a stool and "shake hands" when he was a four-month-old colt! All it took was a little grain and a lot of practice. Over and over she stood him on the stool, rewarding him with oats. It didn't take long for him to catch on. The way to Magic's heart was straight through his stomach!

Jenny closed the stall door tightly behind her and latched it carefully. Then she slipped between the fence rails and hurried across the yard.

She still had the rabbits to feed and water, and it was starting to get dark. It was almost time for dinner. Jenny knew she'd better hurry. Dad had been grumpy lately. Soon he would be looking for her, and his mood would not be good. Even though she knew he was grumpy because he had lost his job, it was still hard to understand. It was unlike him to be grumpy, but now he snapped at her all the time.

Jenny entered the rabbit pen, opened a cage, and slipped out a food bowl. Reaching into the feed can, she scooped some feed into the bowl then put it back into Hoppity's cage. The water bowl was still full from the morning, so she moved on to the next rabbit.

She moved down the line, caring for each of her bunnies one by one. Just last week Mom had come into Jenny's room late, just to talk. "There's no need for you to fret," she'd told Jenny. "Your dad will find work quick enough. Things will get better. I promise."

Jenny shoved a food bowl into Frostine's cage, then moved on to Thumper. After pulling on each cage door to double-check that it was locked, she turned to go.

Mokey, the barn cat, came trotting down the sidewalk, meowing and rubbing against Jenny's legs. She stopped to pet the orange-and-black-marbled cat. Mokey wove in and out of Jenny's legs, purring as she stroked her.

"Jenny!" Mom called sharply.

"I'm coming, Mom!" Jenny answered.

"Well, hurry up! Why do you always lollygag? It's almost dark!"

Jenny sighed and told herself to be patient. Things would get better. Mom had promised.

Springer met Jenny at the backdoor, his tail wagging so hard that his whole body wiggled. Grinning, Jenny scratched her dog's head and knelt down to kiss him on the nose. He was a black-and-white Border collie mix they had rescued from the pound.

Inside, Dad was sitting at the kitchen table. His elbows were on the newspaper spread out before him. With his head in his hands, he scanned the classified section. Mom was at the counter making sandwiches.

"Dinner is almost ready," she said softly.

Jenny wrestled with Springer on the way in the door. "Come on boy! Speak to me! Speak!"

"Jenny!" A dark expression exploded on Dad's face as he looked up. "Can't you ever come in the house quietly? I'm trying to read the paper, and all I get is a lot of racket."

Jenny felt the tears stinging her eyes. She hadn't meant to be noisy.

Mom patted her shoulder. "He's worried," she whispered, then handed Jenny a plate with a ham-and-cheese sandwich and a few chips. "Why don't you go into the living room and let Dad look for a job in peace?"

Grasping the plate, Jenny headed for the other room with Springer following her. When she turned on the television set, he sat down and rested his head on her knee.

"Do you love me, Springer? Or is it my sandwich that you love?"

Springer cocked his head to the side and whined an answer as she began to watch cartoons. She was so engrossed in the show that she didn't hear her mom come in.

"Jenny? Don't you have a book or something you can read?"

"I guess, but I'd rather watch cartoons."

"I think you'd better read," Mom said in that

same soft voice. "Your father's worried about all the bills we have coming, and the noise from these silly shows could make him crabbier."

"Cartoons aren't silly!" Jenny protested. "I can't believe you won't let me watch TV!"

"Oh, Jenny! Please don't argue with me! We have enough problems as it is. If your father doesn't find a job soon, we could lose everything!"

"What do you mean?" Jenny bit her lip.

Mom sank down on the couch and pushed a strand of long brown hair away from her face. "It's been over half a year now. I thought your father would have another job quickly, but it just hasn't happened. Now we all have to pull together to keep from losing it."

"Losing what?" Jenny bit her lip again.

"Everything, honey. The farm, the house, the animals—everything."

Pulling Springer close to her leg, Jenny wrapped her arms around him. "But, how? You said everything would be OK!"

"I thought it would be. But we're three months behind on our house payments, and we have a stack of bills four inches high on the desk. As if that weren't enough, your father hasn't even had one call from the jobs he has been interviewed for. My part-time job at the grocery store just isn't enough."

"What are we going to do?" Jenny whispered. "We can't lose the farm!" She thought about Magic and Mokey, her special cat. And what about the rabbits?

"Daddy will find work," Mom said determinedly. "We just have to give it a little more time. Meanwhile you have to do your part. You're eight years old now, old enough to understand. It would help if you didn't complain. And let's try not to watch too much television. Every little bit helps."

"Okay," she mumbled. "I'll try."

Springer reached up and licked Jenny's face, now wet with tears. She buried her head in the fluff of his neck as Mom left the room.

It just couldn't happen, Jenny decided. Daddy

had to find a job. They couldn't lose everything. She could never part with Magic. She'd raised him from a colt. She couldn't part with her rabbits either. They were her 4-H project. She loved and needed them!

Springer wiggled a little closer, eyeing the half-eaten sandwich on Jenny's plate. She slipped it to him, and he swallowed it in one gulp, begging for more. Jenny's appetite was gone.

She looked down at her wonderful dog, and suddenly she realized she could lose him, too!

two

"You don't think they're serious, do you?" Molly asked, her eyes wide with worry. "I mean, you couldn't really lose the farm, could you?"

"Yes," Jenny answered slowly. "Mom was pretty upset."

Molly reached over and grabbed her best friend's hand. She hiked her blue-and-white book bag up on her shoulder, and kicked a path through the leaves in the trail. "Your dad just has to find a job," she said. "I can't even think about you moving away!"

"I know. Me either."

"It won't get that far. He'll find a job real soon."

"Maybe . . ." Jenny's voice trailed off as they came to the split in the meadow path. Molly would take the path the rest of the way up the hill to her house, while Jenny took the gravel drive that ran behind the pasture. From her house on top of the hill Molly could look down on the whole valley, even on Jenny's farmhouse with Magic's three-acre pasture and the long, low building that was the rabbitry.

"Well, see ya," Molly said.

"Yeah. Meet you at the bus stop in the morning."

"Call me if you want to talk," Molly said.

Jenny nodded. She stood still, watching her friend walk up the hill, her long, blonde curls spilling over the collar of her sweater. Then she turned onto the gravel drive. Mrs. Henshaw's yard was weedy and overgrown, with milkweed plants filling the back lot.

The caterpillars. She'd almost forgotten about the caterpillars.

Ever since she was small Jenny had come to the milkweed patch in late September to collect tiny caterpillars with brightly colored black, yellow, and white pinstripes. Mom and Dad had brought Jenny to the milkweed patch even before she started kindergarten. They taught her all about the caterpillars, and Jenny always took a few home to put inside her bug box. And every year it was the same. Each caterpillar would eat until it was big. Then it would hang by its tail from the box lid, or sometimes high on a milkweed stem. Dad explained that the caterpillar was spinning a chrysalis. Even though it was hard to see, Jenny knew the caterpillar was pulling tiny strings around itself until it was enclosed in its own tiny world—warm and safe within its cocoon.

Inside, a transformation would take place, and within two weeks a bright orange-and-black monarch butterfly would emerge. Every year it happened like clockwork. It was one of the things Jenny could count on.

She started kindergarten the next year and took a caterpillar to her class. The teacher put it inside a big aquarium with a lid. As the caterpillar spun its chrysalis, the class gathered around to see. Two weeks later, when the butterfly came out, Jenny felt so important! The teacher took the class outside, and they cheered as Jenny released it.

Jenny stepped off the gravel road and into the milkweed patch. Kneeling down, she peered up at the plants' undersides. She searched the stems and leaves. When she saw a half-eaten leaf and some tiny black droppings, she knew a caterpillar was nearby. Then she saw one chewing on a broad green leaf. And just above, on a bigger leaf, was another one.

Grasping a thick stalk, she broke off a milkweed stem. Sticky white liquid oozed out of the stem and dripped down her arm. Jenny opened her lunch box, laid the milkweed plant inside and added some extra leaves. Carefully she picked up one of the light colored caterpillars with the yellow and black stripes and placed it on top of the leaves.

Even if things were all topsy-turvy at home, the caterpillar would be the same. It would eat and spin and come out all beautiful just when it was supposed to. Jenny carefully carried the box up the lane.

When she reached the pony pasture, Jenny crawled between the fence rails. She balanced the open lunch box in her right hand while trying to control the book bag swinging on her left arm. Magic whinnied and came trotting across the field as if to say hello. She pushed him away with her shoulder.

"Not now, boy," she said. "You're going to knock me over or make me drop something."

Magic shoved his nose at the lunch box, trying to lip up a large green leaf that was sticking out the top.

"No, boy!" she yelled. "These are not for you!"

Magic jerked his head back, alarmed at Jenny's tone.

"Sorry, boy," she whispered. "I still love you!" Jenny crawled through the rails on the other side of the pasture and into her back yard. She reached through the fence and patted Magic's nose to reassure him, the book bag thumping against the rails.

She hurried down the back sidewalk and into the house.

"Mom! Where are you? Dad? I'm home!" she shouted.

The house echoed her words. Jenny hurried through the kitchen and dining room, dropping the book bag in the living room. Voices drifted in from the front porch. She swung the door open excitedly.

A tall, slender woman in a brown jacket was hammering a sign into the front yard. Dad stood on the porch watching, his arm draped across Mom's shoulders. He leaned against her, and the tired look on his face made Jenny scared. She'd never seen her father look so sad before. Mom's arm was wrapped around his waist.

Jenny backed into the living room and shut the door. They hadn't seen or heard her. She was glad. Jenny ran up the stairs and into her bedroom. She sat on the bed, the lunch box still in her hands. The caterpillar was on the top leaf now, inching its way across.

Jenny plunked the whole mess down on her bed and stood up. She didn't want to look, but she had to.

She needed to know what the sign said and why her father looked as if he might cry.

Standing at the window, she drew aside the ruffled yellow curtains. Mom and Dad were in the yard now with the woman, and they were talking. The woman's jacket hung down in front of the sign, so Jenny couldn't read it. The woman shaded her eyes and looked up.

Jenny jumped behind the curtain. She felt wrong to watch even though she knew she had to. So she sat on her bed and watched the caterpillar crawl up the milkweed stalk to a new leaf.

A moment later, when she looked again, the woman was getting into her car and Mom and Dad were nowhere in sight.

The sign was facing the street. Jenny had to tilt her head to read it, and after she did she wished she hadn't. It said:

FOR SALE: 4 ACRE FARMETTE. . . . RAINBOW REALTY, PAULA MARTEN, AGENT, 555-7701.

three

Why did things have to be so complicated? Why did Daddy have to lose his job? Jenny knew that a lot of people who worked with her dad at Miranda Industries had been laid off. But, why her dad?

Jenny picked up the milkweed leaf, and the caterpillar crawled onto her finger. It tickled, but she didn't smile.

She could hear Mom and Dad talking at the dining room table. Their voices were a low hum—a sad sort of drone. Jenny knew she should go down, let them know she was home, and that she knew about the house. But she wasn't ready yet.

The thought of selling their house was scary. It was also confusing, because it wasn't happening the way Mom had explained it would. Mom had said if they got too many payments behind, the bank would take the farm away. So why had her parents hired someone to sell it? How could they do that?

Opening her closet door, Jenny crawled inside and felt around on the floor. On top of a stack of games she found her bug box. She crawled out and filled the box with the milkweed plant, standing it up carefully just like it grew in the field. Then she laid the caterpillar on a broad leaf and snapped the lid closed. She placed the box on top of her dresser where the sunlight could shine on it, and turned to go down stairs.

When she entered the kitchen, Mom motioned

for her to sit down. "Hi, kiddo. We heard you rustling around up there. How was your day?"

Jenny didn't answer. She sat down in the chair next to her mother.

Dad gazed at her blankly, then spoke. "Honey, we have to talk," he said.

"I know," Jenny answered. "You're selling the house." All at once she was angry. The tears burned behind her eyes. She tried to hold them in, but it was impossible. "How could you do it?" she blurted. "How could you just give up like that?"

Dad's hand covered hers in an instant. "We didn't want to," he said, and Jenny could see the sadness reflected in his eyes. "But if we don't sell the place ourselves, the bank will take it. At least this way we can pay them back and save some of the money for another home someday."

"Where will we go?"

There was a moment of silence before Mom answered. "Do you remember Miss Libby?"

Jenny could just barely remember the woman who

used to visit before Grandma had died. But she did remember a little, like how the woman's eyes sparkled when she smiled, and how her grey hair was always rolled into a bun.

"Yes."

"Well, Miss Libby still lives in town. A few years ago she had her house remodeled into two big apartments. She lives in one of them, and a man named Mr. Bertrand lives in the other side."

"So what's that got to do with us?"

"Let me finish," Mom said. Dad squeezed Jenny's hand and nodded. "Mr. Bertrand was having trouble getting around on his own, so he made arrangements to go into a retirement home. I saw Miss Libby in town yesterday. She said we could rent his half of the house if we wanted to."

"Is that where we'll move?" Jenny asked flatly.

"Yes."

"When?"

"Mr. Bertrand is moving into the retirement home in two weeks. We'll move in shortly after that."

"But, what about the animals?"

Mom stood up and wrapped her arms around Jenny. She held her daughter close. "I'm so sorry honey. We can't take them with us."

Jenny's shoulders began to shake, and she was overcome with fear. "But where will they go?" she pressed.

The silence seemed to surround the three of them, its emptiness echoing throughout the kitchen. Mom's voice cracked when she finally spoke. "They'll have to be sold or given away, Jenny. There is no other way."

Jenny's hand curled into a fist, and she lifted it into the air. At first she wanted to strike out at someone—anyone. Her mind was screaming. How? How oh how could this have happened? It just wasn't fair! She pressed her face into Mom's warm shoulder, and the anger drained away leaving an awful ache in its place. Then the sobs came, shuddering through her in waves. She felt Springer's warm tongue licking her hand, and she crumbled to the floor, her arms wound tightly around his neck.

"Not Springer?" she pleaded. "You can't take away Springer!" Mom and Dad joined her on the cold hardwood floor.

"No," Dad said. "Not Springer. Miss Libby said he could come too."

Jenny wanted to say thanks, but she couldn't. The words wouldn't come. It was hard to be thankful when she was losing so much. So she just buried her head deeper into the scruff of Springer's neck and let his fur catch the tears.

Later that night, lying in bed, Jenny watched the caterpillar in its bug box on top of the dresser. The night-light cast an eerie glow over it. The caterpillar was munching leaves contentedly. Already it seemed bigger than before. Jenny knew it would soon hang by its tail and prepare to make a chrysalis. The chrysalis would be its new home. Jenny wondered if caterpillars ever worried about leaving their whole world behind?

four

Jenny led Magic through the gate, then climbed up on his back. He seemed to sense her sadness, and turned his head to nudge her knee. "It's OK, Magic," she whispered, but the tears burned a path down her face.

She nudged him gently. He plodded down the path, then out onto the gravel road behind his pasture. Springer tagged along, his long, pink tongue hanging out the side of his mouth as he trotted to keep up.

"You see," Jenny explained to her pony, "you are going to live at your new home. Everyone at the top of the hill has been looking down at you for so long. Now it's your turn to live at the top of the hill and keep watch over the valley."

Jenny rubbed Magic's neck softly. "You can keep an eye on the house. You can see who moves in and whether they take care of everything or not. Then when I come to visit you, I'll ask, 'Hey, Magic, is everything on the farm still safe? Is the grass still trimmed neatly?' In the spring I'll ask, 'Are the flowers in my flower beds coming up like they always do?' You'll feel safe because at least you'll be close to home. At least you aren't going to a strange place."

Jenny swallowed hard to keep from crying again. "You know Molly! Don't you, old boy? Soon you'll love her as much as you love me."

Jenny wrapped her arms around Magic's neck

and lay over him with her face in his scruffy mane. She wanted to be mad at Molly for taking her pony away, but how could she when it had been her own idea? Besides, Molly had always wanted a pony of her own, and she had always loved Magic. She had known him since he first came to live on the farm as a colt, had seen him do his first trick and give his first ride.

Mom and Dad had told Jenny that she was lucky the summer grass had lasted so long. With the cost of winter hay, Magic would have been sent away long ago if it weren't for the grass that grew free.

Mom and Dad had talked about running an ad in the paper to sell him. Then they talked about taking him to the auction barn. But Jenny couldn't bear the thought of not knowing where he would go, or who would have him. What if his new owners were unkind? That was when Jenny thought about Molly. Her parents knew and trusted Molly. Maybe if Jenny offered to give Magic to her, Molly's parents would say yes to a pony for her. Now Molly was waiting for

Magic to come be her pony.

Two weeks had gone by so fast. Mr. Bertrand had moved out of Miss Libby's house, and now it was ready for them. The boxes were packed and waiting to go. Mokey had found a home after being advertised in the paper under the column that read FREE ITEMS. The rabbits had been given away to members of Jenny's 4-H rabbit club. She knew they would be taken care of. They would be shown, too, and if she went to the shows she could see them again.

The last one to go was Magic. Jenny wanted to deliver him by herself. Partly to have this last ride alone. Partly to be able to tell him good-bye and explain why they had to move.

Jenny guided Magic on the gravel drive that led up the hill to Molly's house. The sky was clear blue, and the autumn leaves on the trees below the skyline were bright with color. The sun was warm and the day was beautiful. If only it weren't Jenny and Magic's last ride together.

"Hello!" Molly's voice floated down the hill,

ghost-like. Springer barked with joy and hurried to greet her. Molly waved and ran down the hill to meet them.

The new house was pretty, Jenny had to admit. It was an old, white, farm-style house with brick halfway up on the outside. Dark red shutters framed each set of windows. Colorful mums of purple, pink, rust, and yellow spread out lazily around the front porch steps, and crisp white ones lined the walk. The grass was neatly trimmed, and there were two doors leading inside from the front porch. Miss Libby lived on one side. The movers carried boxes of the Freelys' belongings through the other door.

Mom buzzed around like a bee, telling the workers where to put the furniture and boxes, and offering cans of soda. Every now and then she would breeze by Jenny, patting her on the head before going on to the next task.

Jenny wished Mom didn't look so cheerful. She wished she could be cheerful.

"Jenny, want to go with me to get Springer?" Dad asked. Jenny hadn't seen him walk up behind her. He didn't look cheerful either. Maybe he felt like she did.

"OK," Jenny answered. Anything was better than watching the confusion here.

She followed her dad to the pickup truck and climbed onto the seat. Buckling her seat belt, she stared out the window as they backed down the driveway. She noticed a girl who looked about her age playing in the yard next door. She also noticed the little general store, just three doors down from the house in town. Most of all, she noticed that there were no horses or cows or rabbits or rolling hills. Just four rows of houses, a general store with a gas pump in front, a bank, and a post office. Just town.

They rode home in silence. Jenny was lost in thought. What would it be like, living in town?

The farm-house was empty, and it echoed a protest when they entered. All the life had left with their boxes of belongings. Springer wiggled and licked Jenny's face, happy that she was home.

He followed them out the door, unaware that he would not return. Jenny squared her shoulders and closed the door firmly behind her. Dad drove the truck out the driveway and down the road toward town. Springer sat beside her on the seat, wagging his tail unknowingly. Jenny didn't look back.

five

The bug box was on top of the dresser, just like it had been at their old home. It was the same dresser, too. Jenny and her mom had even arranged the bedroom furniture in the same way in Jenny's new bedroom. Except for the desk. It couldn't be in the same place because there was a big window with a seat along that wall. Jenny plunked herself down on the faded cushions and leaned back against the curtains. She stared at the bug box.

The caterpillar was munching a circular pattern around the edge of a big half-eaten milkweed leaf. It had more than doubled in size, and was now the size of Jenny's index finger. The caterpillar didn't seem to mind that the Freelys had moved.

Jenny pulled her knees up to her chest and spun around. She pushed aside the curtains and looked down at the big back yard below. It was long and narrow, lined with hedges on one side and along the back. There was a walk leading to a pretty screened building. Jenny knew that the little round building with fence-like sides and a fancy three-tier roof was called a gazebo, because her aunt had one just like it in her back yard. She remembered that the benches inside were a perfect place to read a book or be alone. At least there was one good thing about this place.

Jenny studied the property. She was glad they had moved on the weekend. At least she would have time to get used to her new home before starting a new school on Monday. From the window, Jenny could see many trees. The oaks were tall and majestic. There were dogwoods and poplars and maples that looked perfect for climbing. Jenny jumped up impulsively. She had never climbed a tree before. The few trees they had on the farm were too small dogwoods or hickories, tall and spindly with the branches way up high. She trotted down the stairs.

Jenny stepped out into the brisk autumn air with Springer trailing behind. She looked up at the rainbow of colors swirling down from the canopy of trees while Springer raced around, getting to know his new surroundings. He seemed just as content as he had been on the farm. Maybe to a dog, home was wherever his family was.

Poplars stretched tall and straight, with their branches almost touching the sky. Jenny watched as one by one, leaves dropped to the ground, big and tulip-shaped, and as bright yellow as the afternoon sun. Jenny stopped to pick up a handful of leaves, breathing in the tangy autumn smell. She threw them in the air, and Springer leaped to catch them in his mouth and raced away.

Jenny eyed the big maple tree with orange-yellow leaves drifting down from it. It had a split trunk and two branches that spread out from either side like outstretched arms. She carefully placed her sneaker into the split of the tree and hoisted herself up. Wrapping her arms around the half trunk in a bear hug, she pushed herself upward until she could grab the limb. From there it was easy to slip her legs around the limb and spin her way up.

A wide grin filled Jenny's face. Who would have thought her first time to climb a tree would be after she moved into town! Suddenly Jenny felt like laughing. She had not felt like laughing for weeks—hadn't had a reason to even smile. She still didn't have a reason, but she felt the grin spread across her face anyway. She didn't want to live here, didn't want to be in town without her pony and her cat and rabbits. But there was something about being in the tree that made her feel better. Jenny rested her head against the trunk and surveyed the world below.

The girl she had seen on moving day was in the yard next door. Only a short hedgerow separated the yards. The girl's hair was plaited into two long braids that hung down her back. A big white dog with shaggy hair and a wagging tail stood watching her, his long pink tongue hanging out. The girl was raking leaves, but she wasn't doing it right, Jenny thought. Instead of raking them into piles for jumping into, the girl was raking paths all over the yard. Some of the paths were winding. Some formed big connecting circles that crisscrossed other paths. Others twisted into dead ends that were hidden behind trees.

Jenny studied the patterns as the girl stopped and rested against the rake handle. Springer circled the tree, then jumped up, clawing at the rough bark and whining. He let out a yelp and the girl next door looked at him and then up. She waved and smiled at Jenny. The shaggy dog came bounding across the yard and through a gap in the hedges.

Jenny smiled again. She slid down the tree trunk,

tumbling to the ground breathlessly. By the time she stood up and brushed herself off, the girl and the dog were standing beside her.

Springer and the shaggy dog both bounced with excitement. They chased each other around the yard as the girl spoke. "I saw you yesterday! I'm Susan and I live next door!"

"I'm Jenny. We just moved in."

The girl looked a little like Molly. Her dog stopped to nudge Jenny's hand gently.

"Behave, Bitsy!" Susan ordered the dog.

Jenny laughed. "Her name is Bitsy? But she's huge!"

"Yeah," Susan laughed too. "My mom thought of calling her that! Hey, can you come over and play?"

Jenny hesitated. "I'll have to ask my mom." She turned to run in the house, then remembered something. "What were you raking over there?"

Susan grinned slyly. "They're paths. Everyone is coming to play Catchers on the Path!"

six

Catchers on the Path? Jenny wondered what that could be while she ran inside to see if she could play next door.

When she got to Susan's yard, she meant to ask, but Susan asked about Springer first.

"He's a Border collie and husky mix," Jenny explained. "He loves people!"

"So does Bitsy. We're volunteers with the Pets for

People program. Bitsy and I go to nursing homes to visit people who don't have pets. It's fun!"

"Hey!" Susan said suddenly. "Are you ready to start school on Monday?"

"I don't know. I guess."

"I'll help you find your way around. And you can walk with me to the bus stop," Susan suggested. "We meet on the corner."

"OK," Jenny answered shyly. She didn't even want to think about the new school, but if she had to go, it would be easier going with a friend.

The dogs began to race around the yard, as if playing tag. Then Bitsy dodged between the girls, almost knocking Susan over and leaving her breathless.

"Bitsy!" Susan scolded. "Shame on you!"

The big dog immediately dropped to the ground on her belly, her shaggy head on her paws. She rolled her eyes up at Susan comically, and Jenny began to giggle.

"You say you're sorry!" Susan demanded. Bitsy

answered with a low grumbling bark.

"Okay! You're forgiven," she told the dog. "Go on and play!"

Bitsy jumped up and raced off with Springer again.

Jenny shook her head in wonderment. "Wow! How did you teach Bitsy to do that?"

"She is smart, isn't she?" Susan asked. "I don't know. I guess just lots of love."

"Neat!" Jenny smiled. Then she heard a grunting sound behind her, followed by a wail.

"Get your cow off of me!"

Jenny spun around to see who was talking. A short, chunky boy with dark hair, freckles, and glasses was pushing a pink tongue away from his face. Bitsy had plastered him with a greeting.

"Bitsy!" Susan reprimanded, and the dog sat.

The boy hiked up his baggy pants and pushed his heavy dark glasses up on his nose. Bitsy reached up to plant one last sloppy, wet kiss on his hand. Seeing that he was missing the action, Springer bounded over to add a few kisses of his own.

"Yuck! Call them off!" the kid yelled again.

"Oh, Sammy!" Susan pushed the dogs away and pulled the boy over to where Jenny was standing. "Jenny, this is Sammy. He lives two doors down."

Just behind Sammy, a girl with short, curly blonde hair and sparkling blue eyes arrived. "I'm Lauren," she said quietly.

Susan grabbed Jenny's hand and pulled her closer. "Lauren, this is Jenny. She just moved in next door."

"Hi," Lauren said shyly. Then she turned to Susan. "Are we ready to play Catchers on the Path?"

Jenny sucked in her breath, summoning her courage. "I don't know how," she admitted.

Sammy hiked up his pants and giggled. "It's easy!" he said. "You do know how to play Catchers, don't you?"

"Sure."

"Well, Catchers on the Path is just like playing regular Catchers, except. . ."

"You have to stay on the path!" Susan interrupted.

Sammy put his hands on his hips. "I'm telling her!"

"All right!" Susan rolled her eyes.

"Like Susan said," Sammy continued. "You have to stay on the paths. If you step off the path while you are being chased and the person who is 'it' sees you then you're 'it'."

Jenny looked at the network of paths crisscrossing the yard. "Sounds neat!" she exclaimed. "Where's base?"

Sammy looked at Susan. "You raked them! Where's base?" he asked gruffly.

Susan skipped across the yard, behind a tree, to where she had raked a big square in the grass. "Base," she said. "Now stick out your fists."

Jenny put her fists out with the others and Susan began, "One potato, two potato, three potato, four, five potato, six potato, seven potato, more." Her fist came down firmly on Sammy's tightly clenched one. "You're 'it'!" she screamed, and the three girls raced off down the paths, followed by the two rowdy dogs!

Sammy went after Lauren, so Jenny slowed to catch her breath and watch the chase. Springer paused beside her and she gently scratched his head. She thought about Susan and Lauren and Sammy. Having neighbors was sort of neat.

Something Susan had said stuck in Jenny's mind. Pets for People—what was it? Tomorrow she would have to find out more about it from Susan. Maybe it was something she and Springer could do too.

That night, Jenny sat on the edge of her bed. Traffic whizzed by outside, and a street light cast its glow across her yellow ruffled bedspread. It wasn't dark and quiet like the country. It was hard to sleep. Springer seemed untouched by it all, though. He was curled in the corner of the room, snoring softly.

Jenny thought about the farm and wondered who might live there next. She thought about the new house in town and the friends she'd made already. Then she heard Dad's words in her mind. "When one door closes, another one opens." Maybe it was true. She had found new friends, and she liked the long tree-filled back yard here. But still . . .

The bug box on top of the dresser was faintly lit by the street light. Jenny flipped on the light and padded over to check it. The caterpillar was hanging by its tail, its body shaped like a U. Jenny knew it was spinning a chrysalis, pulling tiny unseen threads around itself, building a new home.

seven

Jenny woke up on Monday morning before her alarm rang. Her first day at the new school was today. She pulled on the clothes she had laid out the night before. Then she remembered the chrysalis.

Already it was darker in color, almost black, with flecks of orange wing showing through the transparent skin. Soon a monarch butterfly would come out.

"Hurry up, slowpoke!" Susan called as Jenny came out on the front porch. "The bus will be here any minute! You don't want to miss your first day at my school!"

Jenny pulled her coat tight around herself, feeling a blast of cold air lift up the collar then flap it down again. She felt her cheeks flushing and she knew it wasn't just the sudden drop in temperature. Maybe she *did* want to miss her first day at Susan's school! Her stomach lurched at the thought of a strange new place and halls full of kids she didn't know.

Nevertheless, Jenny hurried down the steps and began the short walk to the bus stop.

"Worried?" Susan asked.

"A little. I won't know anyone."

"You'll know me," Susan answered in a hurt voice.

Jenny smiled at her new friend and brightened a little. "Yes! I know you, and I'm awfully glad I do."

The roar of an engine drew their attention to the

yellow bus that was rounding the bend in the street, red lights flashing. Jenny grabbed Susan's hand, and they raced to catch the bus.

When the last bell rang, Jenny walked to the bus. The bitter cold of morning was gone, and although the air was still a little brisk, the sun was warm.

On the bus ride home, Jenny sat between Lauren and Susan.

"How did you like your first day at our school?" Lauren asked in that quiet little voice she had.

"It was OK. My teacher's nice, and I sit next to a girl named Terri. She has a horse named Buster, and she lent me a pencil."

"Long red hair and freckles?" Susan asked. Jenny nodded. "That's Terri Stonesifer. She's really nice."

"Everyone was friendly, but lunch was just as awful as it was at my old school!"

Lauren giggled, and Susan put her finger in her mouth, stuck out her tongue, and made a gagging noise. Jenny and Lauren laughed even louder.

"The only thing that was different and I didn't like," Jenny added, "was staying in all day. At my old school we could go out on the playground after we finished our lunch."

"Wow!" Susan sat on the edge of the seat. "You were lucky. We only get to go out three times a week for gym. I think tomorrow is your class's day."

The bus brakes whined as the driver pulled up to their stop. The doors whooshed open. After all her worrying, Jenny smiled. The day had gone so quickly!

Jenny could smell dinner cooking before she even got to the kitchen. It was roast beef with carrots, potatoes, celery, and onions—and it smelled delicious. Daddy was there, wearing a grey suit and a tie. He was smiling.

"How was your first day of school?" he asked.

"It's alright. I met a new girl and I rode to and from school with Susan."

Dad smiled. "That's super, honey!"

"So why are you dressed up?" she asked.

"We're celebrating two things," Mom said. "Ms.

Marten called. She found a buyer for the farm!"

Jenny's smile faded. How could that be a reason to celebrate? She sat down slowly. "What else are we celebrating?" she asked quietly.

"I had a job interview today," Dad said proudly. "It was the second time they called me back, and it went very well, if I do say so myself."

"I spent too much money on the roast," Mom said. "But we have new hopes!"

"Do you really think you'll get the job?"

Dad shook his head. "I don't know. But I'm a firm believer that when one door closes, another one opens."

"If he does get it," Mom explained, "Daddy will be managing a department in a shoe factory."

Jenny looked down. "You shouldn't have sold our home. If you already have a job, we could have kept the farm! You shouldn't have sold it!"

"Oh, honey! I know it seems that way, but we were too far behind in our bills to ever catch up without selling. Even if Daddy does get the job, we couldn't have kept the farm."

Daddy patted Jenny's hand. "We have to look forward now, not back. Someday, we'll have another place in the country. It won't be the same, but it will be ours."

Jenny wanted to believe the words she heard, but she just couldn't. Not anymore. There would be no new home in the country, no special farm. They would probably live here, in town, forever. She missed Magic's soft nuzzling kisses, the feel of his warm furry neck against her cheek when she was down and out. She missed galloping through the pasture, the wind burning tears in her eyes. She'd never do that again. Somehow she just knew.

eight

Squeak, squeak, squeak. The porch swing outside the living room window whispered a squeaky tune as it swayed . . . back and forth . . . back and forth. Jenny lifted the drapes and peered out to see who was swinging.

"It's Miss Libby," Mom called from the hallway cheerily. "Why don't you go out and say hi? She hasn't seen you in such a long time!"

Miss Libby was a tiny woman. Her toes barely touched the floor, pushing off to keep the swing moving. Her grey hair was rolled in a bun just like Jenny remembered, and the few wisps of hair that had fallen from the sides rose and fell with the rhythm of the swing.

Jenny slipped on a jacket and went outside. The storm door slammed behind her. The day was unseasonably warm. Jenny sat down on the front porch step, watching Miss Libby on the swing. Her wire rim glasses didn't hide the intense green eyes that were lost in thought.

"Pretty day, isn't it?"

Jenny was surprised when Miss Libby spoke. She remembered a thin, birdlike voice. But Miss Libby's voice was raspy and deep.

"Yes." She smiled at Miss Libby.

"When I was young like you, I used to love days like this. Tree climbing days, they are. It's a running barefoot-through-the-fields-with-your-dog kind of day. Now, the best I can do is pump this old swing until the wind brushes my face. Then I close my eyes and remember the breezes high up in those rustling branches, and the warm sun feeling its way through to touch me here and there on my arm or face. Oh, I remember those days."

Jenny squirmed on the step. She felt a little uncomfortable, as if Miss Libby wasn't talking to her at all, but to herself about some far away remembered day. But another part of Jenny felt warm because she could picture herself up in that tree, and it was neat that an old lady could still feel like that. She looked up to find Miss Libby studying her face, and she blushed.

"I've seen you in that old tree," she admitted. "Did you think an old lady like me had forgotten how it feels to be young?"

Jenny shook her head.

Miss Libby lowered her voice. "We never forget," she said softly. "We have so much locked inside our minds to share."

Jenny shifted uncomfortably, then looked up

again. "It was nice of you to let us stay here. And to let me bring my dog," she added.

"Shucks, girl. It's good to have some young blood next door. Makes me feel young again!"

"You are young, Miss Libby!"

"Some folks say you're as young as you feel. Well, if that's true I'm pretty young today. But some days I'm right old." Miss Libby's eyes sparkled as she spoke, and she did look young. Jenny couldn't guess her age.

"That dog's mighty special to you, isn't he?" Miss Libby crooked her finger toward Springer who lay at Jenny's feet.

"Yes, he is."

"You should join the Pets for People program with Susan and her dog."

It was the second time Jenny had heard about this program. Now she was really curious. "What is the Pets for People program?" she asked.

"It's such a nice thing they do. Those people all get together and take their pets to visit with the old people at the retirement home. Some of them haven't been near an animal since they went into the home. Some of them miss their own pets so much they cry for them. But Pets for People takes away some of that hurt by letting them hold and pet the dogs and cats. Sometimes they even bring along a little bunny or a singing canary!"

Jenny closed her eyes. She could picture a room full of elderly people with kittens and puppies on their laps and a cage with a canary in it, singing away. It was a nice picture.

"I'd like to do that," she said softly. She didn't think Miss Libby heard her, but she did.

"You could do that Jenny. You and your dog could do that."

Jenny was very still on her bed. She was thinking about the talk she and Miss Libby had had. Miss Libby was right. Springer was more than a dog. He was a friend too. Sleeping in his corner on his rug, he seemed as peaceful here as he had been on the farm.

Jenny thought about Magic. He was her friend too. She still wanted him back so much that it hurt. She wondered how he was.

Jenny went downstairs and picked up the phone. Carefully, she dialed Molly's phone number. She wanted to hear her old friend's voice, and she needed to find out about Magic.

Jenny cradled the receiver against her ear, listening to the shrill ring on the other end. Finally, Molly answered.

"Hi. It's me," Jenny said quietly.

"Jenny!" Molly squealed into the line. "How are you? How do you like living in town?"

Jenny smiled in the dark. "It's OK," she answered. "The neighbor, Susan, is my age. She has a neat dog."

"I miss you," Molly said. "And Magic misses you too!"

"I miss you guys."

"Magic sometimes stands in his stall, with his head hanging over the door, gazing down at the farm.

He looks like he's keeping an eye on things. It's weird!"

Jenny remembered her last talk with Magic, and she smiled. Maybe he had understood. "Maybe he is!" she told Molly. "Have you been riding him?"

"Yeah. We ride all around the farm and on the same trails you did. Thank you for letting me have him, Jenny. You'll always be my very best, best friend."

Jenny smiled again. "You too," she whispered.

After she hung up and padded back upstairs, Jenny sat on the edge of the bed, remembering and missing.

Then she flipped on the light and looked at her bug box. She hurried over to check the caterpillar's progress. The chrysalis had been spun. It was a minty green "finger," hanging from the lid of the box. Jenny knew changes were going on inside. Soon the caterpillar would become a butterfly.

Almost a week had passed since Jenny started at her new school. As she reached home, Jenny thought about how quickly she'd fit in and had gotten used to everything.

Jenny leaped the porch steps two at a time. She dropped her books in the hall and dashed upstairs to check on the caterpillar.

The butterfly had emerged from the chrysalis just as Jenny had expected. Now it clung weakly to the top of a milkweed branch. Its wings were wet and still folded tightly against its body. Jenny knew the monarch needed time to dry out. She watched the new life, holding onto its old home. Tomorrow she would release it. It was a little late in the season for a monarch, but it would lay its eggs on the milkweed plants just the same, then move on. Jenny wondered if the monarch would feel sad and sort of empty in its strange new world. Like she still did sometimes.

"On Monday I start my new job!" Dad announced at dinner. "Just think. Only a couple of days ago you were the little lost puppy dog in a strange new school. I guess that will be me tomorrow—a lost puppy dog in a strange new job."

"Really?" Jenny jumped out of her chair and ran to hug her dad! "You really got the job?" she asked again, even though she knew it was true.

"Yep. But now I'm too scared to go!"

Even though he was smiling, Jenny wondered if her dad really was worried like she had been. "It's not so bad, Dad," she reassured him. "I made a new friend, and my teacher is super. Maybe you'll make a new friend and have a nice boss too."

"And maybe, just maybe, I'll like it even better than my old job. You never can tell! Sometimes a change of scenery is good for us all."

nine

Inside the bug box, the monarch had crawled from the milkweed branch to the top of the box. Its wings were all dried out, and it fluttered restlessly against the lid of the container. Picking it up carefully, Jenny carried it down the stairs. It was time to release the butterfly, time to let it go find a new life.

"Hey! Where are you heading?" Mom asked.

"I gotta let the monarch go!" Jenny explained. "Susan is meeting me out back."

Mom shook her head. "I guess all this excitement is good. Go ahead!" She waved her hand toward the door.

Susan was waiting in the back yard. "Let me see! Let me see!" she called impatiently.

Jenny held the bug box up so Susan could see the bright, orange-flecked wings fluttering.

"Wow!" she breathed. "Did you really have it since it was a caterpillar?"

"Sure! I found it on the milkweed plants near my old house. Next fall I'll show you. Are there any milkweed plants near here?"

"There's a patch of milkweed behind Sammy's row of houses."

"Let's go there to turn her loose," Jenny suggested.

While they cut through the yards to the back row, Jenny explained: "It'd be lost if I didn't turn it loose near the milkweed plants. That's where they need to lay their eggs for new caterpillars to hatch out."

When they reached the empty lot, Jenny opened the bug box. The butterfly crawled onto the lid, and she stuck out her index finger. The monarch crawled up, leaving whispers of tickles as it made its way to the top of her hand.

Susan reached out to touch the powdered wing lightly. "It's so neat," she said.

Jenny nodded, then lifted her finger high in the air. The setting sun was still warm, but Jenny knew the cool of night would be back soon, and she worried about this late-blooming butterfly.

The monarch flapped its wings slowly one last time, then lifted off, fluttering gently toward the sun. Susan's eyes were sparkling, but Jenny's held a hint of worry. She knew how the monarch must feel as it began its new life.

Jenny whistled as she brushed Springer's hair in short strokes. She fluffed his long tail hairs, then hooked a leash onto his collar. "Ready?" she whispered. Springer cocked his head to the side and whined.

"Susan is here!" Mom announced. Jenny waved her friend into the room, and Bitsy followed.

"The van is waiting outside. Miss Libby is already in the front seat, chattering away." Susan giggled when Mom said this.

Jenny slipped on her jacket. "Ready, captain!" she said with a salute. Under the jokes and smile, she was a little nervous. It would be her first time visiting the Shady Brook Retirement Home with Springer and the Pets for People program.

A cold wind whistled into the house when Jenny opened the front door. Miss Libby was waiting in the front seat of the Pets for People van. Her face was bright with color, and she wore a tall, purple feather in her hat. Jenny knew this was her favorite evening of the week. The Pets for People program always took Miss Libby along to visit her friends.

The driver introduced himself as Jenny climbed into the back seat with Springer. "Hi Jenny. I'm Chuck."

"Hi!" Jenny said as she slid across the seat to

make room for Susan and Bitsy.

"We're glad to have you with us," he added before pulling away from the curb.

Jenny clicked her seat belt tight around herself, then sat back nervously.

After picking up a lady with a tiny Holland Lop bunny and a teenage boy with a cat in a carrier, they arrived at the retirement home. Jenny and Springer followed the others inside. They filed down a dark corridor and into a brightly lit room. A silver-haired lady was playing the piano. She stopped and turned to see what all the commotion was about.

"The recreation room," Susan whispered. Then she waved at a small, stooped man with a gray crew cut. "Hi Mr. Singally! Bitsy missed you!" Indeed, Bitsy was trotting across the room to greet the elderly gentleman.

The silver-haired lady turned back to the piano and began to play "How Much Is That Doggie in the Window?" Other people in chairs, on sofas, and at card tables began to tap their feet in time with the music. But most of the residents were walking over to greet the animals. A tall man with a long green sweater hurried over to gather the cat out of the carrier, while the lady with the lop bunny slipped it into the lap of a woman in a wheelchair.

Jenny stood rooted to her spot by the wall, watching the others. But Springer had other ideas! He wanted to meet everyone, and he whined and tugged Jenny from her spot, across the room to where Miss Libby was visiting with a thin, distinguished looking gentleman.

"This is my friend, Bertrand," Miss Libby said.

"Hi," Jenny said softly for what seemed like the tenth time that day. "This is Springer," she told the gentleman.

"What a beautiful animal." Mr. Bertrand reached down to stroke Springer, and Jenny beamed.

A bald man with a cane waved a pointed finger at Jenny. "Don't bring that animal near me!" he ordered. Jenny looked down quickly and turned back to Mr. Bertrand. Maybe he still isn't used to his new home, Jenny thought. And she understood.

❀ ❀ ❀

The van dropped Jenny and Miss Libby off at their door, and Jenny helped Miss Libby up the steps.

"Well child, what did you think of the Pets for People program?"

"It was great, Miss Libby. You were right about what you said. Some of the people tonight seemed so happy to see all the pets."

"They were waiting on you. They were waiting on the others. You see, there is always something to be happy about in life. To many of the folks at Shady Brook, those pets are a reason to celebrate."

Jenny pondered Miss Libby's words as she held the door open.

"I hope you will go next week too," Miss Libby added.

"I will!" Jenny said. Then she told Miss Libby "goodnight" and went in.

Jenny sat in her window seat and gazed out into the back yard. The round fixture on the top of the gazebo looked like a golden ball, its tip reflecting the moonlight. The yard was a mass of shadows and light. The once pretty trees were now like a crowd of people, short and tall, fat and thin, all waving their stick limbs, casting eerie shadows onto the checkered yard.

Miss Libby had said, "There's always something to be happy about in life." Jenny once thought that all her happiness was tied up with living at the farm. She thought moving would take away her happiness. But she was wrong, and Miss Libby was right.

ten

Bundled up in a winter coat, a scarf wrapped around her neck, and mittens on her hands, Jenny headed outside. The day was gray and cold. Mom was waiting in the car, and Jenny was nervous. She couldn't wait to get going though.

She hadn't slept at all last night. Just thinking about the visit today had kept her awake. It seemed like she'd waited a lifetime, but it had really only been four months since they'd moved away in September. It was almost Christmas and she was getting her Christmas wish. She was going to visit Molly—and Magic!

As they rolled up the long driveway, gravel crunched under the tires loudly and Jenny clutched the presents in her hand. She saw Molly waiting at the window. Then she was at the front door, throwing it wide open before the car had even stopped.

"Jenny! Jenny!" Molly called as she rushed forward to greet her friend. "Gosh, I missed you!" Molly gushed.

Jenny grinned and grabbed her friend's hand tightly in her own mittened one. Then she looked down over the valley at her old farm, her old home, nestled below in the greying afternoon. Looking back at her buddy, Jenny grinned. She realized she missed her friend more than the farm.

"Come on!" Molly squealed. "Magic can't wait to see you. I told him you were coming!"

As they walked to the barn, Molly told Jenny how

lonely it had been without her, and for the first time Jenny realized that the move had probably hurt Molly as much as it had hurt her.

Jenny thought about the last few visits she had made with the Pets for People program. All the folks at the retirement home had moved to be there. Jenny loved being a part of their new lives. She loved bringing them some joy. It was part of her new life now.

"I don't know what I would have done without Magic," Molly said. "He's been everything to me. A pony and a new friend!"

"I guess he was meant to be here with you. I'm so glad you have him."

Jenny entered the barn slowly, taking in everything: the smell of a warm horse, hay, straw, and leather. It was all so good! Then she heard a whinny ring out and there was Magic, thrusting his head under her arm, nuzzling her with his tiny muzzle. Jenny laughed and buried her face in his neck, breathing the horse smell deeply. She stroked his back and ruffled his mane between her fingers. "He knows me, doesn't he?" she laughed. "He really remembers me!"

"Of course he does," Molly said softly. "Old friends always remember each other."

Jenny pulled Molly close, and they both buried their faces in Magic's neck. The pony stood quite still, as if he loved every minute of it!

In the house, Jenny told Molly all about her new school and the house she lived in. They exchanged presents. Molly gave Jenny a brand new bug box, twice the size of the one she already had. Jenny gave Molly a box of writing paper with horses running across the top of each page, and she made her friend promise to write often. Then, they went back out to the barn so Magic could unwrap the bag of carrots from Jenny! She hugged her old friend good-bye.

When they came back out, it was evening and the first snowflakes of the season were falling. Like cold, wet kisses, they landed on her cheeks and nose, but inside Jenny felt warm as toast. She thought about Magic and Molly, Susan and Bitsy. She thought about her new school and the Pets for People program. She thought about Miss Libby, Dad and Mom, and she realized everything was good.

What was it Dad was always saying? "When one door closes, another one opens."

Well, he was right!

Check out these other delightfu
Charming Ponies books!

A Pony to the Rescue

Friends Amanda and Shannon are determined to find out
ghost story they heard is true. But before they can, Shan
must conquer her fear of riding, and a beautiful pony na
Christa might be just what she needs.

A Perfect Pony

It's the most exciting day of Niki's life! She's saved up enough
money to buy her very own pony, and today is the day of the
pony auction. She could take home a magnificent pinto or a
proud thoroughbred, but she sets her heart on a
beautiful white mare instead. When a little black horse with
big sad eyes distracts Niki from the mare of her dreams, will
she miss the chance to own the perfect pony?

A Pony Promise

Tiffany Clark has to keep her big brother's family secret,
it's not easy. Luckily she can confide in Windy, the pinto m
at Mr. Paul's horse farm. But when Windy and a mare nar
Stormy give birth within days of each other, there's a probl
It's going to take a miracle for Stormy's foal to survive,
nothing short of a horse adoption can save the day. Will Wi
agree to raise another mare's foal?

HarperFestival
A Division of HarperCollinsPublishers

www.harpercollinschildrens.c